FIESTA Femenina

Celebrating Women of Mexican Folklore

retold by **Mary-Joan Gerson**

illustrated by **Maya Christina Gonzalez**

Barefoot Books

Step inside a story

Editor's Note:

This book uses the term "Mexican folklore" to refer to
narratives from the wide variety of cultures rooted in the land we now
call Mexico. These narratives are drawn from diverse indigenous, European
and mixed origins. The word "folklore" is an imperfect term, as it can imply
that the stories are not true. This book aims to share these tales with the utmost
respect to their original roots and to those who hold them sacred today.

*Barefoot Books would like to thank Claudia Guadalupe Martinez
for her invaluable input on this revised edition.*

*To the people of Mexico, who have proudly and
generously shared their vibrant culture with me — M-J. G.*

Throughout time … for my Matthew and Sky — M. C. G.

Barefoot Books
Bradford Mill, 23 Bradford Street
West Concord, MA 01742

Barefoot Books
29/30 Fitzroy Square
London, W1T 6LQ

Text copyright © 2001 by Mary-Joan Gerson
Illustrations copyright © 2001 by Maya Christina Gonzalez
The moral rights of Mary-Joan Gerson and Maya Christina Gonzalez have been asserted

First published in the United States of America by Barefoot Books, Inc
and in Great Britain by Barefoot Books, Ltd in 2001
This paperback edition first published in 2021
All rights reserved

Graphic design by Jennie Hoare, England. Cover design by Sarah Soldano, Barefoot Books
Reproduction by Bright Arts, Hong Kong. Printed in China on 100% acid-free paper
This book was typeset in AlcuinEF, Bromello and Giovanni Book
The illustrations were prepared in acrylics

ISBN 978-1-64686-272-6

British Cataloguing-in-Publication Data:
a catalogue record for this book is available from the British Library

Library of Congress Cataloging-in-Publication
Data is available under LCCN 00012965

3 5 7 9 8 6 4 2

Contents

Illustrator's Note 4

Author's Note 6

Rosha and the Sun 8

The Hungry Goddess 12

Tangu Yuh 18

Why the Moon Is Free 24

Green Bird 28

Blancaflor 34

Our Lady of Guadalupe 46

Malintzin of the Mountain 56

Sources 62

Glossary 64

4

Illustrator's Note

My art rises from a deep sense of being and gathering myself together. Even for a book project, art is more ritual than image-making. These stories felt very important to me because they're stories related to my ancestors. They provided one of those opportunities for heart and hand, spirit and story, to dovetail through making art.

The paintings of the stories remind me of my visit to Mexico City and Diego Rivera's murals. I loved his gorgeous fresco style, fresh and raw in both what he painted and how he painted it. These stories felt connected to his murals and our shared past, and I wanted to pay respect to him by incorporating a visual connection. I used acrylic washes on gessoed paper to give a fresco look similar to his murals.

Then there was Frida Kahlo's home and birthplace, Casa Azul, in Coyoacán. Like Frida, I don't separate myself from my work, but instead allow my life and heart to enter the frame. Her spirit must have been particularly strong with me when I was creating one of the illustrations for the "Green Bird" story in this book. This one piece stands out to me, not just from this book, but from all of my books. Like Frida, I love nature and this one reminds me of both her and myself. It was inspired by a photograph of an orangutan parent holding their baby. It embodies everything I hoped to convey: Spirit. Depth. Love. Family. Nature. And similar to much of Frida's work, it evokes longing, loss, hope, endurance. It's very personal, and it's also universal.

Green Bird hangs in my home right now, but has toured in art shows across the country numerous times and been seen by more people than any other piece of art I've made. For me, this painting is the heart at the core of *Fiesta Femenina*. It remains a powerful image to me because it is embedded with all my prayers related to parenthood, from the time I created it to the present day — both good and hard times.

Art is a tool to remind us of who we are, remember our ancestors, heal our present and sing out to the future. Art heals. Make art now.

— *Maya Christina Gonzalez*

☀ Author's Note ☀

In Mexican folklore — meaning, narratives from the wide variety of cultures rooted in the land we now call Mexico — the miraculous is everywhere. From the tallest of the Sierra Madre Mountains, to the tiniest hummingbird, the world is a source of fascination and wonder. In stories where a little mole can save the sun, the most ordinary of characters or events can also prove to be the most extraordinary.

One way in which these narratives represent the extraordinary is through their female characters. Although they do not take the stage as frequently as men, as is the case in many folkloric traditions, women in these stories are extremely powerful. They often possess special talents or traits that enable them to rise above the challenges presented to them. These challenges may come in the form of misguided men, powerful sorcerers or even the Devil himself. But these remarkable women, through their inner strength and creativity, are able to overcome forces of opposition.

I have chosen the stories in *Fiesta Femenina* because they contain unique, powerful female characters and celebrate the indigenous roots of the land now known as Mexico. Some of the women are especially strong, like young Rosha in "Rosha and the Sun," who saves her people when they are cast into eternal darkness. Some are clever, like the Moon in "Why the Moon Is Free," who outwits the Sun when he tries to take her for his own. Our Lady of Guadalupe is a unique figure among Mexican people, as her profound love protects them when no one else can. And Blancaflor and Green Bird show amazing amounts of courage as they fight against oppression to be with the men they love.

I have also included several stories that examine the complexity of women — their ability to embody the opposites and contrasts of their cultures. Malintzin is one of the most controversial and mysterious of all the characters in these stories. In this version, she is both the alleged traitor and protector of her people, a character who has to make tough choices in difficult situations. And Tangu Yuh and the Hungry Goddess are also complex characters, who both give to and take away from the

worlds they inhabit. Tangu Yuh's story also emphasizes the importance of women in the world of commerce and, in particular, the women in the Zapotec community of Tehuantepec, where they have controlled finances and trade and held important positions in local government for many years.

These stories are drawn from a variety of Mexico's rich cultural traditions. Both the Maya and the Aztecs, Mexico's two most historically famous indigenous groups, are represented by the tales of "Rosha and the Sun" (Maya) and "The Hungry Goddess" (Aztec). The tale of the princess Green Bird comes from the Mixtec people, who live in southwestern Mexico. And the Yaqui people, from the northwest, celebrate women in "Why the Moon Is Free." Where I do not note the particular origin of a story, it is because the story has journeyed across so many different areas and people that no one group can claim it as its own. Some of the stories, such as "Blancaflor" and "Our Lady of Guadalupe," reveal a mixture of indigenous culture and the influence of the Spanish, who, led by Hernán Cortés, invaded Mexico in 1519.

So how do we see these stories reflected in the lives of girls and women around the world today? These tales can inspire readers to explore and emulate the strength and power they see in characters like Rosha in her quest to free the Sun, or the Moon in her refusal to let a man's wishes determine her fate. Like these characters, girls and women are working to claim their power and influence in family, cultural and political life all over the world.

— *Mary-Joan Gerson*

Rosha and the Sun

I n a village deep in the green, lush Maya hills lived a brother and sister, named Tup and Rosha. Like many children of the Maya highlands, they had bright red cheeks and dark black hair. Rosha's hair was especially thick and lustrous, hanging like a cornstalk down to her feet.

Since their father and mother were so busy planting corn in their fields, Rosha and Tup often found themselves alone. When they were very little, it was Tup who made up all the games they played. But when they grew older, Rosha had her own ideas, and sometimes she liked to play all alone. This made Tup very angry. He wanted his little sister to do whatever he said.

One day during the harvest season, both their parents went to the village to sell the extra corn they had grown. It was a hot, sticky day, and all the breezes were trapped behind the mountain's wall of trees. Rosha slipped off by herself to dip her burning feet in the bubbling stream behind their house.

Tup, left all alone, got hotter and hotter and angrier and angrier. He looked up at the flaming red ball of sun in the sky and thought of his sister, who was probably cooling herself somewhere nearby. "I will play a game that will be special, and more wonderful than any Rosha has thought of," he said to himself. "I am going to catch the sun, and Rosha will help me do it, whether she wants to or not!"

And that is what he did. The next morning, while Rosha was sleeping, Tup crept towards her very slowly. He was carrying the machete their father used to cut the cornhusks. Rosha's eyes were tightly shut, and her long black hair flowed over her pillow onto the floor. Very quietly and very quickly, Tup sliced the machete across the width of Rosha's hair!

She awoke from her sleep and rubbed her eyes. She tried to shake her hair free of the morning dust and dew, but there was nothing to shake. Where was her hair? She saw her brother standing in the corner grinning slyly at her.

"My hair!" she cried. "What have you done with my hair?"

Tup jumped up and down with glee. "I've made a nest to catch the sun," he cackled.

Rosha ran out of the house, her eyes burning with tears. When she reached the edge of the woods, she saw that everything Tup had said was true. There lay the sun, sputtering with light and heat, tangled and woven into her hair.

"You fool!" she yelled at her brother. "Now we will never see the corn grow again. Now we will be cold and weak from morning till night."

"That will teach you a lesson for ignoring me," laughed Tup.

Rosha tried to free the sun in every way she could. She pulled and pulled at the matted web of her hair. But her hands burned from the sun's fierce flames, and her cheeks were scorched by its glowing heat.

Rosha ran deep into the forest to look for help. First she found a deer munching on leaves. "Will you help me free the sun?" she begged.

"Oh, I couldn't leave the forest in the daytime. It's not safe for me," said the deer.

Rosha ran on and came upon a wild turkey feathering its huge nest. "Please, help me free the sun. It is trapped and dying."

"Don't be silly," sputtered the turkey. "The sun is too grand to be caught for long."

Exhausted and discouraged, Rosha sat down under a mahogany tree, shivering in the cold, sunless morning. A little mole crept along the ground. "Why are you crying?" the mole asked.

"I am trying to free the sun so that we can grow food again," she said. "And no one is brave enough to help."

"I am very brave," the mole said boldly. "I will help you."

Rosha smiled in the midst of her tears and stroked the mole's little head. She wondered how so tiny a creature could be so bold.

"Oh, little mole, I am sure you are brave beyond words, but a tiny creature like you can hardly help free something as giant as the sun." She noticed that the little mole was shivering with cold, so she picked it up and wrapped it in her shawl.

The mole snuggled deep against Rosha's side, and her steady step soon sent him into a deep sleep. Then he had the most wonderful dream. In the dream he was a powerful hero, larger and stronger than every animal of the forest.

Before long, Rosha saw the blazing, sputtering light of the captured sun. When she approached it, the mole jumped out of her shawl. Filled with the power of his dream, he crept up to the strands of Rosha's hair and jumped inside them to snip them with his sharp teeth. The brave little mole jumped up and down, and snipped and snipped. He was so quick that before the sun could scorch his feet or face, he had loosened all the threads of Rosha's knotted hair.

Then in one giant flame, the sun rose out of the nest and sailed back upwards into the sky.

From high above, the grateful sun showered its light on Rosha and the little mole. Then its booming voice echoed through the deep green valley. This is what it said:

"To you, mole, I promise a safe shelter in the forest. From this day forward, you will be able to live underground where no other creature can harm you."

"And for you, young Rosha, who saved my light for all the world, I promise this: Your eyes, and the eyes of all the Maya women, will shine with my golden light forever."

The sun kept its promise. If you watch carefully, you can sometimes see a mole slither down into a deep hole whenever it encounters danger. But you don't have to look carefully to see the light that flashes in the eyes of Maya women everywhere, thanks to Rosha's determination.

The Hungry Goddess

In the time before dawn, the Aztec gods lived in the heavens. High above, where the gods lived, there was only empty air. There was no sky and no earth. There were no birds and no clouds and no breezes. And down below there was only water. There was water everywhere. The water steamed in the summer and froze in the winter and splashed in between. Everything was wet and soupy.

Among the gods there lived a goddess. Her name was Tlaltecuhtli, the Hungry Goddess, because she had eyes and mouths all over her body. She had mouths and eyes on her back, on her fingers and even on her toes — everywhere! She was always hungry, always trying to eat. She was always crying out, "I am hungry! I am hungry!"

In the morning she wailed, "I am hungry."

In the evening she screamed, "I am hungry."

And worst of all, all night long she wailed and screamed, "I am hungry!"

The other gods couldn't stand the noise. They couldn't sleep. They couldn't think. "What can we do?" they wondered. Tlaloc, god of rain and lightning, had an idea. "We will present our problem to Quetzalcóatl and Tezcatlipoca, the most powerful among us. Surely they will have a solution."

They marched together to these two most powerful gods and begged, "Please, you have to help us. We cannot sleep and we cannot think. You must stop her from

wailing all day and all night."

Quetzalcóatl was also called the Plumed Serpent because he wore feathers of every shade of the rainbow and carried a magic stick in the shape of a serpent. He wore a mask with an eagle's face. From the mouth of the eagle he could blow the wind all across the world.

Tezcatlipoca wore rattlesnakes around his legs. On his foot he had a magic black mirror in which he could see everything that was happening — anywhere!

Quetzalcóatl and Tezcatlipoca talked and talked. It was springtime and they decided they would take Tlaltecuhtli, the Hungry Goddess, down to the water. After all, she didn't seem happy living among them in the thin, empty air on top of the world. Perhaps the sound of the rushing waves would soothe her.

So Quetzalcóatl swept the Hungry Goddess up onto his gigantic wingspan. Tezcatlipoca wound the rattlesnakes on his legs around her body to keep her fastened, and they dove down to the frothy edge of the water's current.

"I am hungry!" she cried. "I am hungry!"

First the gods gently laid the Hungry Goddess on the water so that she would become accustomed to its cold, salty surface. She was so quiet. She floated and paddled and seemed quite content.

The gods said, "Ah, she is so happy here. She must no longer be hungry."

But no. She started to cry out again: "I am hungry!"

The noise was too much for Quetzalcóatl and Tezcatlipoca to bear.

Quetzalcóatl blew the water to the left and to the right. He blew it up and down. He dove deep into the heaving sea, trying to find something the Hungry Goddess could eat, but there was nothing in sight. Tezcatlipoca searched the edge of the water for a hundred miles for a sign of life, but he found none. The sea was cold and wavy and deep, but it was empty.

Quetzalcóatl and Tezcatlipoca were very disturbed. "What will the other gods think if she returns unchanged?" they wondered. "We, the most powerful, have been asked to solve this problem. We cannot fail!"

And so Quetzalcóatl and Tezcatlipoca turned themselves into huge snakes and took hold of the Hungry Goddess. "We will stretch out her body so that she will no longer feel so hungry," they thought.

They pulled and pulled her. But she was very strong and fought them with all her might. Lightning flashed in the sky, and the ocean heaved and roiled from their struggle. It was the most difficult challenge the gods had ever faced. Then all of a sudden — by accident — they snapped her in half.

Everything was silent. Quetzalcóatl and Tezcatlipoca gazed at each other in shock. What had they done? They had destroyed a goddess! They had broken her in half! Quetzalcóatl picked up the bottom half of the Hungry Goddess, and Tezcatlipoca picked up the top half, and they carried the pieces back to the heavens.

They summoned the other gods before them. "Brothers, look at the terrible thing we have done," they said.

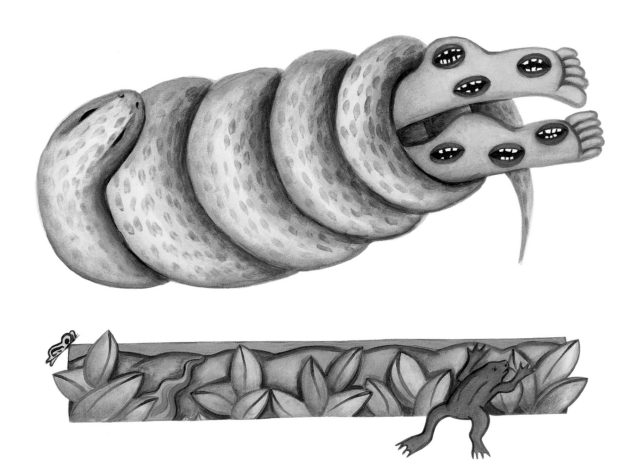

First, the gods covered their eyes in horror. Then one god said, "I have an idea. Let's use her bottom half to make a cover for the world." And that is how the sky came to be.

Then the gods looked at the Hungry Goddess's top half. "Poor Tlaltecuhtli. Look at how sad her face is," one said. "What can we do? If only we could make her happy."

All of a sudden, the gods had an answer. They decided that everything necessary for human life would come from the body of the Hungry Goddess. They changed her hair into a forest teeming with animals and her eyes into the meadows. Her mouth became springs and rivers, bursting with fish and frogs. From her skin grew grasses and flowers. Caves formed from her nose. Her hips became the mountains, and her stomach the valleys.

The Hungry Goddess became Mother Earth, the earth we live on to this day.

The gods sighed, "Ah, she must be so happy. What good work we have done." They smiled and congratulated each other.

But they spoke too soon. They didn't know how hungry the Hungry Goddess really was. Softly from the top of the mountains, and then louder from the inside of the caves, and loudest from the darkest reaches of the forest, came the sound of wailing: "I am hungryyyy, I am hungryyyy!" And it never stopped.

To this day the Hungry Goddess, Mother Earth, is still very hungry and very thirsty. She knows that the seas are full and the forests are thick with trees, but her belly feels empty. When it rains, she swallows all the water. When the sand gets washed into the ocean, she eats it. When the leaves fall and rot, she gobbles them up. When anything goes into the earth, she devours it. She is always starving.

Sometimes, when the night is very still and everyone else is fast asleep, if you listen very carefully, you might hear the cry of the Hungry Goddess. "I am hungryyyy, I am hungryyyy, I am hungryyyy," she calls, eating and drinking and creating the earth while we rest in our beds.

Tangu Yuh

In Tehuantepec, deep in the south of Mexico, there is a toy made especially for the New Year — a little clay figure of the goddess Tangu Yuh. She is dressed just like the Zapotec women who live in Tehuantepec because she wears a wide ruffled skirt over a white petticoat and *huipil*, a richly embroidered blouse. Her braids, laced with bright ribbon, are piled on top of her head like a crown. Her eyes are glistening black, her lips are as red as tomatoes, and her arms reach out to draw you close.

Do you know why Tangu Yuh is special to the people of Tehuantepec on New Year's Day? Because she once visited them on that day, long ago. At that time, all the Zapotecs lived very happily together. They helped each other in everything, from working on their farms to building their houses.

There were always three parts of their land: north, middle and south. Now, as then, the women of the north wove beautiful cloth, which they embroidered with silken thread. The northern men were famous hunters of iguana, deer and wild boar.

The people of the south were the artists of Tehuantepec. Both women and men worked with clay and wood. They carved pots, and also drums and flutes, which they played all evening long. Right in the middle of Tehuantepec were the traders.

The women of the middle ran the markets. And it was the men of the middle who carried the weavings and the skins made by the northerners to lands high over the mountains. There, they exchanged them for the bright green pottery and carved gourds that the Zapotecs loved so much.

For the most part, the Zapotecs lived their lives in peace and cooperation. But there is always trouble, even in paradise. The problem for the Zapotecs was that no one in Tehuantepec felt really special. The potters in the south often thought, "Our bowls are beautiful, but so is the cloth the northerners weave." The people in the middle would say to each other, "Why do we have to travel so far to trade the goods made by our brothers and sisters? Are we their servants?"

But in the heavens, the gods beamed at the harmony and the peacefulness of Tehuantepec. They couldn't see from so far away that there were dark thoughts and angry feelings inside the people's minds and hearts. The gods decided that the Zapotecs should be blessed with a visit from them, and they selected Tangu Yuh to represent them.

Thus, long ago, something wondrous happened to the people of Tehuantepec at the dawn of the New Year. Just as the children were turning over in their beds, and their parents were trudging out of doors to prepare their breakfast, flashes of lightning streaked through the sky. But instead of the thunder, which usually rings out during the storms of Mexico, heavenly music drifted downwards towards the earth. Suddenly, strange creatures with giant wings of silver feathers filled the sky. They were playing trumpets as long as bamboo trees. A powerful voice echoed through the heavens announcing that a goddess wanted to visit the most contented people on earth.

It was Tangu Yuh! She was so beautiful, with her flowing dark hair and her glistening velvet skirt. Divinely beautiful! She was so beautiful that no one could describe her.

The people from the north were astonished to see that the goddess wore a dress like the dresses they wore to their own celebrations. But her dress shone like gold and blazed with light. They crowded around her, studying the design of her dress, hoping to weave it into their memories. If they could weave cloth like that, how spectacular they would look!

Across the hills and valleys, the trumpet calls reached the people of the middle next. Tangu Yuh flew across the valley sky to appear before them. They could not believe that the goddess was speaking to them in their own language! What heavenly truth could she tell them about their trading? If they listened to the advice of a goddess, they would become the richest people on earth! Everyone from the middle shouted questions at Tangu Yuh all at once. A clatter of noise hurtled upwards to heaven. No one could hear anything at all.

Finally, she descended upon the people of the south. The southerners ran to gather their musical instruments so that they could greet the goddess with blasting trumpets and heavenly melodies. They gathered in the middle of the village and blew with all their might. Surely, Tangu Yuh would see that people on earth could make music like the gods! Some blew so much breath into their flutes that they fainted on

the ground. Some beat their drums so hard that they broke their drumsticks in half. They lined up in procession and marched towards the goddess. "Look! There come the people from the south, with music!" said those of the north and middle. "What took them so long?"

Tangu Yuh saw the confusion she had caused. "Is this the land of harmony and peace I came to praise?" she asked herself. She was very disappointed and very angry. She gathered the heavenly creatures around her, and they flew straight up through the clouds.

By the time the southerners reached the gathering, the goddess had already returned to heaven. The people from the south were miserable. They had barely seen Tangu Yuh before she vanished, and they pounded the others with questions. "What was she like? How were her eyes? Her voice? What did she say?"

But the northerners had tried so hard to copy the design of her clothes that they hadn't really looked at Tangu Yuh. And the people from the middle had shouted so many questions at her, that they never noticed whether she had answered them.

Gloom settled over the land of Tehuantepec. The looms fell silent, and the clay ovens were empty. The Zapotecs, who always laughed and who loved to sing, grew sadder and sadder. They watched and waited for many days, hoping Tangu Yuh would return. But she didn't. And so everyone started working again. The northerners began to weave, but their cloth became just a little more beautiful because of the vision of Tangu Yuh. The people in the middle went back to their trade, but they were a little more generous because they felt blessed by the goddess. And the people of the south created a song, which they set to a soft, sad melody. They taught it to the people of the north and middle:

> Goddess of the earth,
> What would I not give to have seen your eyes?
> What would I not give to have seen your eyes?
> Goddess of the earth!

Time passed, and the people no longer talked of the goddess to their children. It was as if she were a dream, which had floated through the night. But each year on New Year's Day, everyone gathered together and sang the song of Tangu Yuh slowly and mournfully.

High in the sky, the gods heard the song and watched the people of Tehuantepec. They saw that the northerners wove cloth for everyone. They saw that the people from the middle traded for all the others. They were not convinced that another visit from Tangu Yuh would be any different from the last. But Tangu Yuh thought it would. "Let us keep their hope alive," she said.

So the next New Year's morning, when no one expected it, the music of heavenly trumpets blasted in all the town squares, and a booming voice arose from the middle of every village. "Tangu Yuh! Tangu Yuh!" it cried, and the echo of the voice reached all the corners of heaven and earth. What joy the Zapotecs felt! Without a second to lose, they began to plan a *fiesta* in her name, the grandest celebration they could imagine.

Since then, the spirit of Tangu Yuh is with them on every New Year's Day, when her *fiesta* is celebrated. Long before the New Year, the northerners begin to weave new clothes. The traders in the middle bring new foods to eat from across the mountains. Each year the southerners compose new music for the Tangu Yuh chorus. But most of all, the southern potters make new clay figures of the goddess. There is a hush that falls when the clay figures are taken out of the ovens. Everyone in the north, middle and south believes that when the potters truly capture the face of Tangu Yuh, she will visit them again.

When she does come back, they will have her *fiesta* all ready. There will be a brass band leading a winding procession. Banners will fly from every roof and flowers will fall from every window. There will be chocolate and sweet bread to eat, *mescal* to drink and lots of dancing. Everything and everyone will celebrate Tangu Yuh. Surely, she will come again.

Why the Moon Is Free

O h, how the Sun loved the Moon. She was so luminous and lovely. Sun longed to have her for his wife.

"You are more beautiful than the wispy clouds and more shapely than the roundest rose. I want you for my very own," said Sun.

Moon was used to shining all alone at night, and she rather liked it that way. If she ever grew lonely there were a million stars she could talk to, meteors to race against and planets to make her laugh.

So Moon replied, "I will marry you, Sun, with this condition. You must give me a gift of beautiful clothing. I love dresses covered with stitching. I love white blouses with borders of ribbon. And I love long skirts, which float in the night wind. Anything suits me, but it must be exactly my size!"

Even though he was tired from heating the earth and lighting the sky all day, Sun stayed up all night gazing at Moon, trying to choose his gift. He couldn't decide.

"You must look even more beautiful when you are my wife," said Sun. "I can bring you anything from the earth-world. Please tell me what you wish, my love."

"It doesn't matter — a dress, a hat or a woven skirt — as long as it fits!"

"Anything you want," said Sun.

He decided to bring her a skirt woven with golden thread and delicate strips of starlight. "Oh, how all the stars will envy my new bride," Sun thought.

But when Sun saw Moon again, he was shocked to discover that she was only a sliver, a slice of her former self. "Oh, my dear!" he cried. "Love has stolen your appetite. You are looking so thin."

Sun raced across the sky and asked his special tailor to trim the skirt to fit Moon's new long, slender shape.

When he returned, Moon — who was a bit fatter — couldn't slide the skirt over her hips. "Ouch," she said, turning blue from holding her breath and trying to squeeze her moonself into the skirt. "This size is all wrong. This skirt is pinching the light out of me!"

"Oh, my dear, you have become a little plump, but this skirt will fit you perfectly when I return," said Sun.

Sun sped across the mountains and asked lightning to streak the skirt with panels of light so that it would slide down Moon's widened hips.

But by then, Moon was a day or two fatter. She held her breath and pulled her stomach in as far as it would go. "Do you think I am a round tortilla?" she squealed, and her outgoing breath chilled Sun's hot face. "How could you think this skirt would fit?"

For thirty days — all month long — Sun tried and tried, but he could never figure out Moon's shape and size. She was always changing! He would measure her carefully so that whatever he brought would be just right. But whatever it was — a skirt, a hat or a coat — it was too small, or a little too tight, or altogether too big by the time she tried it on.

And so, for this reason, Sun could never marry Moon. Now every day, just before he goes to sleep in the western sky, Sun looks at Moon — who is sometimes slim, often full, and frequently in between, but always glowing with shimmery silver light. And all he can do is gaze at her across the sky when nighttime falls.

And every night, before he goes to sleep, Sun sighs a long, sad sigh of desire denied. And every night, as she slides into the sky, Moon giggles with pleasure and relief.

Green Bird

Long ago, on a day when the wintry sun dropped in the valley of Oaxaca and golden marigolds were scattered across the plain, Great Jaguar, the Zapotec King, decided that his daughter should marry. "Who will suit my daughter, the beautiful and clever young Kesne?" he wondered.

He climbed the narrow stairway of the Temple of Warriors. When he stood at the top of the pyramid, he had a vision of power so great that his eyes were blinded in the sunlight. "Aha!" he cried. "I will choose the son of my rival, Seven Alligators, to marry Kesne. Then he and I will rule together across the broad mountains to the endless sea." He summoned his daughter, Kesne, to the temple.

But Kesne didn't come. She was deep in the valley, lying under a mangrove tree in the garden of a man named Tidacuy. Kesne loved Tidacuy with all her life.

When Great Jaguar heard the news, he sent his lieutenants to storm the garden, and they marched Kesne to her father's side.

"I have decided that you shall marry the son of Seven Alligators. Prepare yourself for the wedding celebration."

Kesne's heart froze, and her body shook with anger.

"No, Papa," she whispered defiantly. "I have pledged my life to Tidacuy and to no other."

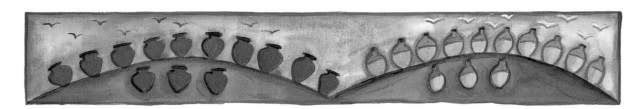

Great Jaguar was stunned. He summoned the court sorcerers to his royal presence. "I order you to punish Kesne with your magic arts," he screamed.

And, indeed, the sorcerers did, changing the rebellious princess into a green bird, with long, glistening feathers. Princess Kesne, now known as Green Bird, flew away from her home forever.

Green Bird felt shame and sorrow about her new form, and hid in the jungle to mourn her disgrace. But the birds of the jungle built a huge bower of branches and leaves to shelter her. Every morning they brought her gifts of flowers from the wildest thickets, and rare and delicious grains to eat.

One day two eagles swooped into the jungle with news. "Great Jaguar has died," they screeched, as they circled Green Bird's hidden home. Deep in her heart, Green Bird had hoped that one day her father would forgive her. Now she realized that she was cursed forever. Green Bird lay on her bed of freshly picked leaves and barely moved.

In the darkness of her palace bedroom, Princess Kesne's mother, Serpent Goddess, heard the news of her husband's death. Since Kesne's banishment from the palace, Serpent Goddess had never let the daylight stream inside to warm her body. She had never opened her windows to the sounds and smells of the earth.

Before Great Jaguar's death, Serpent Goddess had visited the sorcerers many times to ask for potions to bring Kesne back to her, but each time they had turned her away. "A princess who deserts her family is beyond our magic," they told her, but it was really the anger of Great Jaguar that they had always feared.

Now, with Great Jaguar gone, Serpent Goddess appeared again at the sorcerers' chamber. And this time, because they no longer feared his wrath, they revealed the secret of Kesne's enchantment. What's more, they told her that Tidacuy was still waiting for the Princess Kesne, his love for her as strong as ever.

With this knowledge lifting her heart, Serpent Goddess followed a flock of brilliant toucans that led her to Princess Kesne. When she found her daughter deep in the forest, she knelt at her side and said:

"Kesne, my daughter, I have come to find you because your cruel punishment has tormented me. Now the palace wizards have told me how you can once again become a woman, but it is a dangerous thing to undo the magic of the gods. The sorcerers are frightened. They beg us to soften the will of the great and fierce god, Heart of the Sky, so that he does not punish them, and us, for wasting his gifts.

"It will take weeks, perhaps months, to follow their magic commands, and I worry that we may not succeed. Here is what we must prepare: thirteen jars filled with freshly cried tears; thirteen more jars with nectar from every flower in the forest ; and then, a rug woven of feathers in every hue of the rainbow, ten arms long and wide. With these gifts, we hope to soften the anger of Heart of the Sky so that he will hear your prayer."

News of the gifts demanded of Green Bird soon spread throughout the forest, and birds everywhere gathered together in clusters. Soon, they were ready. When Green Bird's mother placed thirteen jars on the highest hill, all the young turtledoves of the forest flew by, weeping and filling the containers with their tears.

And when Serpent Goddess balanced thirteen more jars on the mountainside, an enormous cloud of hummingbirds gathered to collect nectar from every jungle flower. They deposited it, drop by drop.

Finally, parrots and toucans, jackdaws and herons, plucked out their most beautiful feathers with their beaks. They wove them into a dazzling tapestry, which was even ten times larger than the sorcerers had commanded.

With all the gifts in place, Serpent Goddess went to the temple of the gods. She lay face down and then lifted her head to speak to Heart of the Sky.

"Oh, Heart of the Sky! Here are the gifts that Green Bird offers to you so you will set her free! Thirteen jars contain the tears of the turtledoves that have wept over Princess Kesne's disgrace. Thirteen more jars have been filled with the sweetest and rarest nectar. Your most extraordinary birds have plucked out their feathers to create an enormous mat, which covers the steps of this holy place. Let my daughter be free of her father's rageful punishment."

As she spoke, Serpent Goddess's tears flowed from her eyes, and she was bathed in a pool of water filled with flowers. In the heavens, Heart of the Sky, the fiercest of gods, looked down on this mother so determined to save her daughter. He saw that Serpent Goddess was asking nothing for herself, like so many others who cried out to him. Heart of the Sky decided to release the magic, which was his alone to give and to undo.

Suddenly, the sky split with lightning. Deep in the jungle Green Bird woke up to light splashing everywhere. She shook in fear and, as she did, the feathers slid off her body, and she once again became a woman.

Soon after, Princess Kesne was proclaimed the new Queen of the Zapotecs. Tidacuy, her king, stood at her side. Their palace garden was filled with the sound of birdsong. And Serpent Goddess particularly enjoyed sitting in their sun-bathed garden, listening to the birds calling out to each other, announcing the news of the forest.

Blancaflor

Once there was a man named Pedro who was a terrible gambler. He worked hard all day, but try as he might, he couldn't stop himself from gambling all night. He would bet anything and everything. He usually lost. Finally, he had nothing left — no money, no house, no farm. One night, on his way home, grumbling and grouching, he looked up at the moon and said, "I would sell myself to the Devil for a little more money to play cards with."

Immediately, there reared up before him a man cloaked in black on a horse snorting with fury.

"I am the Devil," he said. "What is your wish?"

"Money in my pocket and five years of perfect luck, that's all," replied Pedro.

"Granted," said the Devil. "But in five years' time you are to travel to my house, where I will give you three commands to obey. You will find me on the Plains of Berlin at the Hacienda of Qui-quiri-quí."

Well, from that moment on, every time he gambled, Pedro played with the Devil's luck. Everything he touched turned to riches. He had a big house, hundreds of acres of land, thousands of head of cattle, and all the gold he wanted. But at the end of five years, he knew he had to face the Devil again and settle his account.

He gathered provisions and the strongest horse he could find, and set forth for the Plains of Berlin. Within one month's riding, he reached the ocean's edge. He sighted a deserted house, and when he entered it, he found an old hermit warming his bones in front of a small fire.

"Good day, sir," said Pedro. "I'm looking for the Plains of Berlin and the Hacienda of Qui-quiri-quí."

"I have lived in this desert for one hundred years," said the hermit, "and I have never heard of that place. However, since I am ruler of the fish of the sea, I shall call them and ask them the way to the Plains of Berlin and the Hacienda de Qui-quiri-quí."

From the old hermit's mouth came a screeching whistle and, in an instant, all the fish rose to the surface of the sea.

"Friends, where are the Plains of Berlin and the Hacienda of Qui-quiri-quí?" asked the hermit.

Not one fish could answer.

"Twenty days from here lives my brother, who is even older than I," said the hermit. "Surely, he will be able to help you."

Pedro rode for twenty days and finally reached the brother's house, deep in the rainforest.

"I am searching for the Plains of Berlin and the Hacienda of Qui-quiri-quí," said Pedro.

"I have lived here for more than one hundred years," said the hermit, "and I have never heard of that place. However, since I rule over the animals of the earth, I shall call them and ask them the way to the Plains of Berlin and the Hacienda of Qui-quiri-quí."

The hermit drew in his breath and, with all his might, blew out a piercing whistle. All the animals of the forest and of the mountains and of the plains gathered before his door. But none of them had an answer. The next morning, the hermit called for the lion, his special messenger.

"We have one more brother, who lives deep in the desert. Maybe he can help you." Pedro mounted the lion's back and, holding on tight to his mane, they set out for the desert for the third and last hermitage.

"Hello, good sir," the oldest hermit said, when they arrived at his doorstep. "What brings you to this dry and lonely place?"

"I'm looking for the Plains of Berlin and the Hacienda of Qui-quiri-quí," answered Pedro.

"I've lived here for five hundred years," said the hermit, "and I've never heard of that place. However, since I rule over the birds of the air, I shall call them and ask them to help."

His dry, shrill whistle cracked the thin air of the desert sky. Birds of every hue and feather appeared before him, but when he named and counted them, he saw that the eagle was missing. The hermit whistled again and again, and at the fourth call, the eagle swooped down before its ruler.

"Yes, master?" said the eagle. "I heard you calling, but I was far, far away on the Plains of Berlin near the Hacienda of Qui-quiri-quí."

"Aha!" said the hermit. "Tomorrow, mount the back of this king of birds, and you will reach your destination."

The next morning, Pedro sailed high over the mountains on the strong back of the eagle. As they approached the Devil's house, the sky became wild and stormy. But the eagle told Pedro not to be afraid as they landed on the ground. "If you follow my instructions, you have no reason to fear," he said.

"Look to your right, at that beautiful pond in the distance. Wait there until three doves come to bathe. They are really three beautiful girls. The first two will arrive together. Don't speak to them. They will leave, and a third will come all alone. She is the youngest and the most special of the Devil's daughters. Her name is Blancaflor. You must find a way to talk to her because she can help you."

Sure enough, two doves flew gracefully down to the water's edge and, in a blinking of an eye, their feathers fell off their bodies as they dove deep into the pond. Pedro did as he was told and remained silent as they changed back into doves and flew into the clouds. Then a delicate white dove gracefully landed. The dove began to sing, and her feathers fell around her like flower petals.

Pedro was enchanted by her singing, and he couldn't stop himself from joining her song. Blancaflor turned around and, instead of being startled, she grinned broadly at him. "You have a beautiful voice, sir," she said.

Before long, Pedro told Blancaflor his story, how his rotten fortune had turned to gold and why he had come to the Plains of Berlin. Blancaflor's eyes became downcast and started to tear. With great sadness, she told him how much evil she had seen in her life as the Devil's daughter. "I don't want you to be abused and tricked like all the others," she said.

"I will help you win the struggle with my father and mother. They won't know that I am helping you because they think I'm locked in my room at night behind seven iron locks. My father and mother do not know that with one magic breath, I can open each of the locks and fly into the night."

Blancaflor told Pedro exactly what to do. "Don't take anything my father offers you. When he invites you into his mansion, say you prefer a dirty little shack near the animals' corral. When he offers you some delicious food, say you prefer tortillas that are old and hard."

Just then the Devil appeared. "Good day, my friend. Welcome to our house. Come and join us."

"No, thank you," said Pedro. "I'd feel more comfortable in a dirty little hut near the cows."

"Oh, but come and have some food, friend."

"No, thank you. I am not used to fine food. My stomach will not stand it. I prefer tortillas that are old and dry."

"Very well," said the Devil, thinking this Pedro was quite a strange fellow.

"But you'd better eat and rest well. For in three days, I shall make the first of my three demands of you."

On the third night, the Devil appeared at the entrance to Pedro's hut. He pointed his long, spindly finger straight ahead of him.

"I have come with my first command. Behold that mountain in the distance. At midnight pick it up and place it right next to my house. I want it in my garden."

Pedro ran to Blancaflor. "What will I do?" he cried. "Only a magician could move that mountain!"

"Oh, but I am a magician," she said. As the clock struck midnight, Blancaflor waved her arm, and the mountain waved back. She lifted her arm, and the mountain rose into the clouds and landed right next to the Devil's house.

At dawn, the Devil came out of his house and was amazed. "Look, he has done it!" the Devil cried to his wife.

"I would think this is the work of our daughter, Blancaflor," she replied, "but it is impossible. Blancaflor was locked in her room all night. The seven keys on my waist have not been touched."

Then the Devil returned to Pedro and said, "Prepare yourself for my second special request. I have a great desire to bathe the moment I get out of bed. Tonight you will bring the pond, which lies next to the cornfield, right into my house. I want to dip my toes in the water as soon as I wake up tomorrow morning. Use this basket to carry it," he said, and he laughed a long, dry laugh.

Pedro thought this was truly an impossible demand. He raced to Blancaflor to declare his defeat.

"Be calm, my friend," she said. "Don't worry. I will do it for you."

That night, when everyone was asleep, Blancaflor went down to the pond, and with her long skirt, she swept the water right up to her father's bedside.

When the Devil awoke, he was shocked to find the water bubbling at the side of his bed.

"Look," the Devil called to his wife, "he has brought the pond right into our bedroom."

"If it weren't for my faith in the locks and seven keys," said the Devil's wife, "I would say that Blancaflor had done this work."

The Devil's next command was for Pedro to mount a horse that had never been ridden. "This I can do without your help," said Pedro to Blancaflor.

She laughed so hard she fell off her work stool. "No, no, you will need my help. The horse will not be an ordinary horse but the Devil himself! This is what you must

do. When you go into the stable, there will be spurs, a saddle and a bridle on some hooks. Kick the spurs away from you, for they are my sisters. Don't touch the saddle, because it will be my mother. And be careful with the bridle, because it will be me. Take the big club in the corner, and every time the horse kicks and jumps, hit it on the head with all your might. The club will be magic."

Pedro had never ridden a horse without spurs, but he kicked them across the stable as soon as he entered. He made a long circle around the saddle and bridle, making sure not to touch them. And as for the horse, sure enough, the animal did every devilish jump it could. But Pedro held on tight and hit it on the head with the club. At the end of three hours, a bedraggled, sweating animal was led back into the stable, and Pedro went to the house to find the Devil.

"My master is sick in bed with a battered head," said a servant. "He will see you later."

"Now my father will be very, very angry," said Blancaflor. "We must escape immediately." She unlocked the seven locks of her room as only she could, took a

few of her belongings, and spat three times on the floor. She and Pedro jumped on her horse and rode off into the wind.

The Devil's wife was the first to be suspicious. She ran to Blancaflor's room and called her name.

"Good morning, Mother," answered the three drops of saliva that had come out of Blancaflor's mouth.

When Blancaflor did not appear for lunch, her mother called again.

"Good afternoon, Mother. I am not very well," answered the spittle, but much fainter, because it was nearly dry.

When Blancaflor did not appear at dinner, her mother stormed over to her room.

"Blancaflor, come out of there immediately," she shouted.

"Good evening, Mother. I am ill," whispered the saliva, almost dry.

The Devil's wife pulled the keys off her waist, opened all seven locks, and entered the darkened room. Blancaflor was gone.

Putting together what had happened, Blancaflor's mother became enraged, and she called to the Devil. "Hurry, let us go after them!" They mounted their horses and charged over the plains. There in the distance, they spotted their victims. The Devil and his wife were almost about to catch up with Pedro and Blancaflor, who were riding on only one horse, and it had grown very, very tired.

When she saw her mother and father almost upon them, Blancaflor reached into her bag and pulled out her hairbrush. She threw it over her shoulder, and as soon as it touched the ground, it turned into a thorny thicket. But the Devil made his way through the thicket and almost caught up with them. Just as he was upon them, Blancaflor reached into her bag for her mirror and threw it on the ground. Immediately, it formed a large lake. The Devil and his wife had to leave their horses on the shore and swim across the lake to reach Blancaflor.

The Devil was exhausted and lay down to rest, but his wife pressed on. Soon she came to the house of a little old man resting in the sun. "Hello! Have you seen a man and a woman ride this way?" she asked.

"Watermelons and cantaloupes," he answered.

The Devil's wife turned red. "I said, have you seen two people riding one horse today?" she asked again.

"Corn and potatoes," he answered, for Blancaflor had used her magic on his tongue so that nothing he said would make any sense at all.

Finally the Devil's wife, wet and tired to the bone, also gave up the search.

Pedro and Blancaflor had a picnic on the other side of the lake. "My village is very near here," he said. "I will go home to tell everyone about you, and then I will return to take you to meet them," he said.

"That will be wonderful!" said Blancaflor. "But I warn you. Don't kiss or embrace anyone. If you do, you will forget all about me. This is the curse of being the daughter of the Devil."

Pedro entered his village. He refused to hug his mother, though she was overjoyed to see him. He wouldn't kiss his sisters after they ran up to him and jumped all over him with excitement. But when his old grandmother approached and held her arms out to him, his heart melted with love, and he forgot all about his promise to Blancaflor. As he brought his arms around her, Blancaflor vanished from his memory.

Poor Blancaflor. She waited until sunset, and then she fell asleep on the side of the road. When she awoke the following morning, she realized that the Devil's curse had struck her.

What could she do? Blancaflor sat under a mangrove tree and thought and thought. The villagers noticed her and offered her food to eat. They wondered who this beautiful young woman was, and where she had come from, but then they went about their own business and forgot about Blancaflor as well.

Three days later, there was only one thing on every person's mind in the village. There was going to be a grand celebration for Pedro's return! Every single person in the village was invited. Among all the guests, who poured into the family's compound, was a beautiful young woman, who was carrying a silver tray on which were perched two doves.

Pedro admired the girl from a distance but then turned away to greet his friends. The girl approached him and said, "Little doves, tell the story of Blancaflor and the

forgotten promise."

Everyone listened as the birds chirped and cooed. But they were magical birds, and soon they began telling the story of the Devil, his wife, the pond, the horse, the combs, the spittle and everything else that Pedro had known with Blancaflor. Pedro's eyes were wide with wonder, and he said, "Thank you. That is a remarkable story you have told. But it is not my story, and I must get back to greeting my guests."

Then the girl smiled and began singing, herself. In an instant, Pedro's eyes glazed over, and he remembered the pond in the forest, the two doves who approached and the beautiful Blancaflor, who changed from the dove into his magical rescuer.

"Blancaflor," he cried, now recognizing her standing before him. He fell on his knees and begged her forgiveness.

"No need to beg me," she said, "but I would like to marry you."

Pedro and Blancaflor were married, and they lived very happily together. Pedro never gambled again. He and Blancaflor loved to sing together, when they worked and when they rested. And do you know what? Sometimes, when Blancaflor really wanted something very badly, she still used her magic powers. After all, she was the Devil's daughter, and she had learned some very, very special tricks!

Our Lady of Guadalupe

The legend of Our Lady of Guadalupe began long ago, in the year 1531. One day, just as dawn was breaking, a humble man named Juan Diego left his home to go to church. He was named Cuauhtlatoatzin when he was born, but had taken the name Juan Diego recently, after the Spanish invaded his town. He was just learning to be a Christian, and it still felt a little new to him. Before the invasion, the indigenous people had their own religion and worshipped many powerful gods and goddesses. But the Spanish forbade them to observe their religion and destroyed all their temples.

Thus, when Juan Diego knelt in church and felt a little strange, he always added a special prayer of his own. "Please," he begged, "we are strangers to you. We are just learning this faith. Help us to find our way."

On that December morning, as usual, Juan Diego passed the barren hill of Tepeyac, on which nothing grew except wiry shrubs and prickly cacti. Scattered all around were the stones that had once formed the Temple of Tonantzin, Mother of Corn and Mother of Earth. As he crossed the most deserted area on the side of the hill, he was startled to hear beautiful music drifting towards him, the hills and valleys echoing every note.

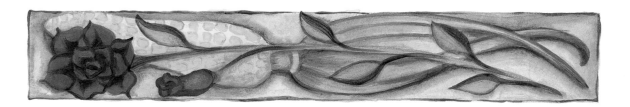

"Is this a dream? Am I walking in my sleep? Our ancestors spoke of a land in heaven filled with flowers and music. Am I there?" Juan Diego wondered.

He crossed himself, for he had learned to do this, and the singing became suddenly quieter. Then he heard a voice calling him:

"Juan Diego!"

He shook with fear, but he forced himself to put one foot in front of the other and climb the hill. When he reached the top, he was amazed. Stretching across the top of Tepeyac was an arc of light radiating every shade of the rainbow. The light shone from a woman with brown skin and hair, like the women in his village, but dressed in flowing robes. Her face was framed by a shawl woven of golden threads. And the brilliance of the light surrounding her even pierced the rock she stood on, so that it glowed like fire.

"My son," she whispered, speaking in Nahuatl, his native language. "Come closer to me."

He drew nearer and fell upon his knees, for now he realized that she was the Holy Virgin.

"Juan Diego, where are you going?"

"O Holy Mother," he answered. "I am on my way to your house, the church of Tlatelolco. The priests there have been teaching us about your religion."

"Listen carefully, my son," she said. "I am the Virgin, Saint Mary, Life Giver, Creator and First Mother. Go to the bishop and tell him that I want a church to be built for me on this hill of Tepeyac. Once it is built, I will protect the people of Mexico forever." Suddenly, the arc of light dimmed and faded. In an instant, the Virgin was gone.

Juan Diego set out for Mexico City to call on Bishop Fray Juan de Zumárraga. As the journey went on, he became more and more frightened. How could a humble man like him visit the bishop? What if he didn't believe his story? Would the bishop even speak Nahuatl, his own language?

Juan Diego was frightened enough to turn back, but each time he thought of doing so, the light of the Virgin appeared in the path before him.

Finally, he arrived at the bishop's palace in Mexico City and timidly approached the entrance. The guards looked at his worn face and torn clothes. "Go away, beggar," they shouted. "This is an important place."

Juan Diego didn't go away. "I have come to see the bishop to deliver an important message."

The soldiers laughed. "And what would a beggar have to say that is important to the bishop?" They slapped each other on the back and laughed again.

Juan Diego stood totally still and repeated over and over. "I must see the bishop. I have come all the way from Tepeyac."

He stood there all afternoon and all evening. The evening guards gave him some water to drink, and he fell fast asleep in front of the doorway. Finally, the following morning, he was allowed into the palace, where again he waited many hours. Then the bishop appeared.

Juan Diego told him his story. "And she would like her church built on the hill of Tepeyac," he said, in a strong, determined voice.

The bishop beamed at the poor country peasant. How much he had learned about their religion, and so quickly. "You must come back and see me another day," he said and smiled at Juan Diego.

The journey back was very difficult. He felt that he had failed the Virgin, and all the people of Mexico as well.

As he reached the hill of Tepeyac at dusk, he was startled again by the sound of heavenly music. Then, the Virgin appeared a second time before him.

"Holy Mother, I have failed you," Juan Diego cried. "The bishop thought I was making up a story. I am not worthy of you."

"No, Juan Diego. You are the messenger I have chosen."

"What can I do?" he asked.

"I want you to return to the bishop and repeat the request that I wish to have a church built on this rock in my name. Tell him about me again."

Juan Diego set out with determination for Mexico City. But he found the same cruel guards at the door of the bishop's palace.

"What, do you wish to bother the bishop again? Get away from here!" they shouted.

"But I must speak to him. He will believe me this time, I am sure." The guards and Juan Diego shouted at each other for an hour until the bishop himself heard the commotion and asked to see what was going on.

Once again, Juan Diego told his story. Once more, the bishop was impressed with this man's deep and true faith, but this time he was concerned that Juan Diego had become a bit carried away by it. The bishop didn't want to discourage him — he was such a good example — and so he said, "You must bring me a miraculous sign to prove your story, my dear man. Please wait for a miracle before you return."

"That will keep him at home where he belongs," thought the bishop.

Juan Diego dragged himself all the way back to the hill of Tepeyac. There, once again, the Virgin appeared to him. He told her that the bishop was still unconvinced, and had commanded him to return with proof. The Virgin smiled and said, "If you return here at dawn tomorrow morning, like the morning you first saw me, I will give you something which will make the bishop believe you without any doubt."

Juan Diego could hardly sleep that night. He couldn't wait to march past the guards at the palace and command the bishop's respect. But when he arose the next morning, he was greeted by terrible news. His oldest uncle, who depended on him, was very, very sick with fever. As the morning wore on, his uncle grew weaker and weaker, and when he was close to death, Juan Diego set off to the church in Tlatelolco to find a priest to hear his uncle's last confession. He was afraid of seeing the Virgin because she might delay him, and so he took a route which kept him away from the hill of Tepeyac.

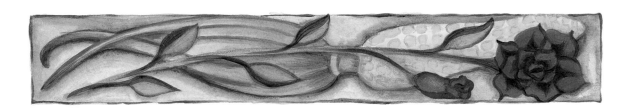

Just as he was nearing his church, he saw the Virgin approaching. He was overcome with guilt for not obeying her orders and fell to the ground to beg her forgiveness.

"Juan Diego, not only are you forgiven for your kindness, but I will restore your uncle to health," she said. "Now go to the hill and bring me all the roses you find there wrapped in your cloak."

Juan Diego's head was spinning in confusion, since roses never grew in December. But when he climbed to the top, he found a garden of luscious roses sprouted everywhere among the cacti. Gathering as many as he could, he wrapped them in the folds of his cloak and raced down the hill to the Virgin.

She took the bundle in her arms and blessed it. Then she told Juan Diego to carry the bundle of flowers to the bishop, but to be certain that no one else opened the cloak to look at the roses. "And tell the bishop again that the Virgin of Guadalupe is going to take care of the indigenous people of Mexico forever."

Juan Diego set off for the third time. But after he had taken only a few steps, he heard a strange sound, like the rippling sound of rushing water. Turning around, he saw that, though the Virgin had disappeared, on the exact spot where she had stood, a spring of clear water had burst out of the ground. With new courage and hope, Juan Diego hurried back to the palace.

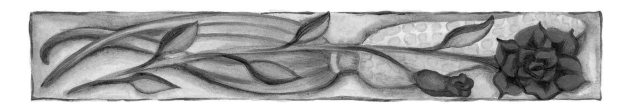

The guards warned him that this was his last chance before the bishop. "One more visit and you will spend a few months in prison, talking to the Virgin," they warned.

Face to face with the bishop, Juan Diego began to speak in a trembling voice. "The Holy Virgin, our Great Mother, appeared again to me, and she bade me gather roses from the hill of Tepeyac, where they have never grown before, and wrap them in my cloak. She promised me that they are proof of her visit, and of her wish for a church dedicated to her, the Virgin of Guadalupe."

"Let me enjoy your roses, dear man," said the bishop, wondering what to do with this confused peasant from the country. As Juan Diego unfolded the cloak, letting the roses fall to the floor, both he and the bishop gasped. They fell on their knees to pray. For on the cloak that Juan Diego had opened was emblazoned the full image of the *Virgen Morena* herself! Her brown eyes and face and her bright shawl gleamed on the cloth, as if she herself were present with them.

The bishop knew he had witnessed a miracle. First, he placed the sacred cloak in a small chapel of the church. That was just the beginning. The following day, accompanied by all the priests of Mexico City, he visited Juan Diego's uncle and witnessed the miraculous cure of his illness.

Then, a long procession climbed the hill of Tepeyac, led by Juan Diego. They stopped at the spot where the Virgin had first spoken to him and where the spring of water now flowed. The bishop and all the priests knelt and prayed to the Virgin. They promised her that a church would be built there, just as she had asked.

As for Juan Diego, he didn't stay in his little village. He spent the rest of his life in a small adobe house next to the Virgin's chapel on Tepeyac. From then on, he carefully guarded the image of the Virgin emblazoned on his cloak, which now hung in a special shrine in the chapel.

Soon, news of the miracle spread throughout all of Mexico. Great crowds of people came to the hill of Tepeyac and were filled with awe at the sight of the sacred cloth.

Now, when December comes each year, pilgrims journey from all over Mexico to visit the hill of Tepeyac, where there stands a huge church called the Basilica of Our Lady of Guadalupe. There are processions and dances. Crosses are taken down from the hill of Tepeyac and freshly painted. On the morning of December 12, before the sun rises, all the pilgrims serenade the Virgin. Fireworks are shot into the air, and at five o'clock the bells announce the celebration of the first mass.

Then, everyone enters the church covered with flowers for the Virgin. On that day, Catholics in Mexico feel especially safe and protected by the spirit of the Lady of Guadalupe. After all, she promised she would protect them, long ago, when she first appeared to Juan Diego on the barren hill of Tepeyac.

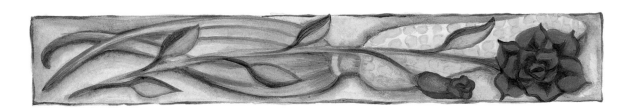

Malintzin of the Mountain

Malintzin was a woman who could talk in many, many languages. And she was very beautiful. She had been born an Aztec princess. But when her father lost all his land in a battle, she was sold into slavery. Her owners were Tabascans, men who traded all over Mexico.

When she became a slave, Malintzin felt that her life was over. She had lost everything. But she had a very strong spirit. In spite of her deep sadness, she learned many languages — Nahuatl, Mixtec and Maya — because her owners had journeyed to so many places. She learned as much as she could, because she remembered that she was a princess, and she dreamed about becoming free again.

When the Spaniards came to Mexico with their thumping horses and gleaming weapons, Malintzin was amazed. She had never seen ships with sails beating in the wind. She had never seen helmets like these, gleaming in the sun. And their pink faces and their long beards? Who were these men? Many of Malintzin's people were very frightened.

But not Malintzin. She was the daughter of kings. The traders sold her as a servant to the chief of the Spaniards, Hernán Cortés. Cortés was determined to conquer all

of Mexico as a prize for his own rulers, the King and Queen of Spain. Before long, as Malintzin worked alongside Cortés and his men, she learned yet another language. She learned Spanish, the language of the strange visitors, and soon she could understand everything they said. Cortés began to see how clever Malintzin was. He began to ask her advice about the land and customs of this new continent he had invaded, and he rewarded her with praise and gifts for her guidance.

But after working with Cortés for many months, something strange came over Malintzin. She decided to help Hernán Cortés conquer the Aztecs — her own people! How could she?

Some people say that Malintzin fell in love with Cortés, and because she loved him so much, she tried to help him in every way she could. But others say that because she was born a princess and had lost everything, she was clever enough to recognize a chance of gaining back her birthright of power and comfort. Still others say that because Malintzin expected Cortés to conquer the Aztecs, she hoped to influence him and make him a kinder ruler. No one knows for sure. We do know that in that time, the Aztec king was Moctezuma. He was a mighty ruler whose every wish

was immediately obeyed. Moctezuma built monuments of stone throughout his kingdom and decorated them with gold and jade and precious jewels.

One day, a messenger arrived in the Aztec court to announce that strangers had arrived in two floating pyramids and were marching towards the city of Tenochtitlán, towards the throne of Moctezuma. All at once, Moctezuma had a vision. In his mind's eye, he saw the great spirit of the god Quetzalcóatl returning to save his people. After all, the Aztecs believed that Quetzalcóatl would return with a white face and long beard. And it was known that Quetzalcóatl had buried his treasure in the mountains. Now he would surely reclaim it. Moctezuma called his swiftest messengers and decked them with the finest jewels and gold, and prepared himself for the arrival of the spirit of Quetzalcóatl.

Hernán Cortés led the Spanish procession of horses and banners into the city of Tenochtitlán, and at his side stood Malintzin. When they arrived at Tenochtitlán, only Malintzin could ask questions for Moctezuma. And only Malintzin could understand the answers. She smiled as she watched Moctezuma present his gifts to Cortés and his men: gold collars and neckbands, flowered necklaces and wreaths for their heads. Malintzin persuaded Moctezuma and all the Aztec nobles to give Cortés everything he asked for. Everything — gold and jewels and fine feathers and chocolate! She helped Cortés trick the Aztecs into surrendering their wealth.

Malintzin didn't see how cruel Cortés was for a very long time. He and his men were never satisfied with their presents. They never had enough. Everybody knows that conquerors are greedy. They wanted to be the kings of this entire land and to have all the people who lived there work for them. They hated the religion and customs of the Aztecs. When Moctezuma finally realized that Hernán Cortés was a heartless visitor from a strange land, and not Quetzalcóatl, his spirit broke.

Before long, the Aztecs refused to accept the increasing demands of the conquerors. The Spaniards, who had horses and guns, put the Aztecs in jail, even Moctezuma. They forced the Aztec nobles to reveal where their treasures were. They killed anyone who refused.

Slowly, Malintzin opened her eyes to Cortés's cruelty. She realized that he would do anything for more gold in his pocket. She felt that she had betrayed her people. She cried and cried, so hard that a river gathered around her and Malintzin floated away from Cortés and his palace. She floated away all alone.

A strong wind came and carried her away to the top of a mountain. The name of the mountain was Texocotepec, which means "the hill where the *tejocote* trees grow" — trees covered with little yellow fruits. But this mountain had fire inside it. There were many caves in Texocotepec, and Malintzin lived deep inside one of them. Every night she cried and cried and pulled at her long black hair. You could hear her in the wind. She cried about all the terrible things that happened to the indigenous people when the Spanish came.

Malintzin lived with the Nahuaques, who had the power to send rain from the clouds to make things grow. Sometimes the Nahuaques got tired and cranky and held back the rain. But Malintzin learned how to soothe their tempers. Inside the Nahuaque caves grew many little plants — squash and tomatoes and baby corn. Malintzin learned how to make ribbons out of corn husks, and she would tie bows of ribbon on these plants — yellow and white and reddish bows. That would make the Nahuaques very happy. They loved ribbon bows. When they saw the bright bows wrapped around their plants, they would beam with pleasure and empty the clouds above Texocotepec.

Malintzin felt that she finally had a home, and the Nahuaques enchanted her. From sunrise to sunset, and during the daylight hours, she was very happy. Every day at twelve noon, when the sun was brightest and the top of the mountain shone like gold, the Nahuaques brought out their golden bugles and giant drums and marched around the top of Texocotepec. Malintzin would join the parade, warming herself in the sun.

Once, a general with many soldiers came very near Texocotepec. He tried to conquer the people who lived in the towns at the base of the mountain. He made all the men and women and little children work all day and all night for him. He treated them like slaves. Then he left, proudly twisting his big black moustache.

Ha! He wasn't fast enough! As he was walking away from Texocotepec, a thunderbolt came down from the mountain and struck him. The general vanished in a wisp of smoke.

How did it happen? They say that from the valley, the people saw a woman covered in jewels sitting cross-legged on the ground where the lightning had struck. She was braiding her long hair, but there were no tears on her face. She was smiling. And the mountain rolled and shook with her laughter.

They say that now Malintzin is a great big woman who wears dozens of necklaces that the Nahuaques have given her — necklaces of coral and jade and amber. And when there is a problem anywhere in Mexico, when the people rise up to fight for their rights, Malintzin calls on the Nahuaques. They blow the bugles of Texocotepec extra loud and beat their drums twice as hard. Their music brings courage and hope to those fighting for justice.

Still, whenever Mexican people are suffering, Malintzin becomes very sad. She still cries and cries. That is why, even when the Nahuaques are angry and hold back the rain which feeds the fields, there is always a carpet of brilliant flowers at the foot of Texocotepec. The flowers can always find water to drink from the pool of Malintzin's overflowing tears.

Sources

Rosha and the Sun

I found this tale in a library collection in San Miguel de Allende, Mexico. The collection was compiled by Ermilio Abreu Gómez, and is entitled *Tales and Legends of the Ancient Yucatan* (Editorial Dante, Mérida, Yucatán, S.A. de C.V., 1993). There is a great deal of wonderful literature on Maya mythology, including James D. Sexton's *Mayan Folktales: Folklore from Lake Atitlán, Guatemala* (Anchor Books, Doubleday Co., New York, 1992); *The People of the Bat*, collected and translated by Robert M. Laughlin and edited by Carol Karasik (Smithsonian Institution Press, Washington D.C., 1988); and Karl Taube's *Aztec and Mayan Myths* (British Museum Press, London, 1993).

The Hungry Goddess

The story of the Hungry Goddess is a basic Aztec creation tale, representing the characteristic coupling of death and life in Mexican mythology. I located versions of this tale in Irene Hamlyn's "The Great Earth Monster" in *Mexican and Central American Mythology* (Paul Hamlyn, London, 1967); Karl Taube's *Aztec and Maya Myths* (see above); and John Bierhorst's *The Hungry Woman: Myths and Legends of the Aztecs* (William Morrow, New York, 1984).

Tangu Yuh

I found this story in Francis Toor's *Treasury of Mexican Folkways* (Crown Publishers, New York, 1947). Another legend that discusses the origin of festivals is "The Origin of Music" in John Bierhorst's *The Hungry Woman* (see above). The Tehuantepec culture is particularly well delineated in Miguel Covarrubias's *Mexico South, The Isthmus of Tehuantepec* (A. A. Knopf, New York, 1946), and in a video documentary, produced and directed by Ellen Osborne and Maureen Gosling, entitled *A Skirt Full of Butterflies* (Film Arts Foundation, San Francisco, California, 1995).

Why the Moon Is Free

The only version of this tale I found was in Ruth Warner Giddings's *Yaqui Myths and Legends* (University of Arizona, Anthropological Papers, Tucson, Arizona, 1959). However, I became familiar with the ideas and beliefs of the Yaqui by reading, in particular, John Bierhorst's *The Mythology of Mexico and Central America* (William Morrow, New York, 1990) and Francis Toor's *Treasury of Mexican Folkways* (see above).

Green Bird

My telling of this story is most closely based on a recorded version I found in a publication while visiting Oaxaca, Mexico, in 1995. The publication is *Myth and Magic: Oaxaca Past and Present*, published by the Palo Alto Cultural Center, Palo Alto, California. The story of a person changed into a bird is a frequent theme in Mexican folklore. Other versions include "The Bird Bride" and "Lord Sun's Bride" in John Bierhorst's *The Monkey's Haircut* (William Morrow & Co., New York, 1986), and "Marikita the Lovely" in Marta Weigle's *Two Guadalupes* (Atlantic City Press, Santa Fe, New Mexico, 1987).

Blancaflor

Blancaflor is a folktale frequently told to illustrate the cunning and power of women. My sources include Olga Loya's *Magic Moments or Momentos mágicos*, with bilingual text (August House, Little Rock, Arkansas, 1997); Riley Aiken's *Mexican Folktales from the Borderland* (Southern Methodist University Press, Dallas, Texas, 1980); and Américo Paredes's *Folktales of Mexico* (University of Chicago Press, Chicago, 1970). A slightly different version of the same story is "Rosalie" in John Bierhorst's *The Monkey's Haircut* (see above).

Our Lady of Guadalupe

The legend of the Virgin of Guadalupe lies at the heart of Mexican culture. I have used several versions of the account for my own telling: Genevieve Barlow and William N. Stivers's *Legends from Mexico or Leyendas de México*, a bilingual edition (National Textbook Company, Lincolnwood, Chicago, 1995), Américo Paredes's *Folktales of Mexico* (see above), E. Adams Davis's *Of the Night Wind's Telling* (University of Oklahoma Press, Norman, Oklahoma, 1946), Olga Loya's *Magic Moments or Momentos mágicos*, with bilingual text (see above), Jacqueline Orsini Dunnington's *Guadalupe, Our Lady of New Mexico* (Museum of New Mexico Press, Santa Fe, New Mexico, 1999) and Ana Castillo's *Goddess of the Americas; La Diosa de las Américas* (Riverhead Books, New York, 1996).

Malintzin of the Mountain

Malintzin is a controversial woman in Mexican history. Some hate her for betraying her people, and others understand how a woman of her time could be misled in her judgment. Just as Moctezuma, the great Aztec emperor, thought that Cortés was a hero instead of an oppressor, so Malintzin fell in love with Cortés, only to eventually realize his cruelty. This version, found in Anita Brenner's *The Boy Who Could Do Anything & Other Mexican Folk Tales* (William R. Scott, Inc., New York, 1946), tells of Malintzin's regret for her mistake and dedication to her people ever since.

I discovered the legend of Malintzin when Marie Brenner told me that her aunt, Anita Brenner, had recorded Mexican folktales in the 1940s, and I was able to locate an edition of this collection. Malintzin's story is also told by John Bierhorst in *The Hungry Woman* (see above) and in Bernal Díaz del Castillo's *The Discovery and Conquest of Mexico, 1517-1521* (Maudslay, A. P., ed., Harper & Brothers, New York and London, 1928). A full perspective on her cultural position is offered by Sandra Messinger Cypess in *La Malinche in Mexican Literature: From History to Myth* (University of Texas Press, Austin, Texas, 1991).

Glossary

Pronunciation Guide to Places and Names

Blancaflor *[Blahn-cah-flor']*
Cuauhtlatoatzin *[Cwaoo-tlah-towah'-tzeen]*
Fray Juan de Zumárraga
  [Fry Hooahn deh Su-mah'-rrah-gah]
Guadalupe *[Gooah-dah-luh'-peh]*
Malintzin *[Mah-lihn'-tsihn]*
Moctezuma *[Mohc-teh-suh'-mah]*
Nahuaques *[Nah-ouah'-quehs]*
Nahuatl *[Nah'-wahtl]*
Oaxaca *[Ooah-hah'-cah]*
Quetzalcóatl *[Ket-sahl-coh'-atl]*
Qui-quiri-quí *[Kee-kee-ree-kee']*

Tangu Yuh *[Tahn'-gooh yooh]*
Tehuantepec *[Teh-wan-teh'-pec]*
Tenochtitlán *[Teh-noh-chit-lahn']*
Texocotepec *[Tex-oh-coh-teh'-pek]*
Tezcatlipoca *[Tes-caht-lih-poh'-cah]*
Tepeyac *[Teh-peh-yahk]*
Tidacuy *[Tee-dah-coo'-ee]*
Tlaltecuhtli *[Tlah-teh-coo'-tlee]*
Tlatelolco *[Tlah-tehl-oh'-coh]*
Tonantzin *[Toh-nahn'-tsin]*
Zapotec *[Zah'-poh-tehk]*

Spanish Words

femenina *[fem-en-ee'-nah]* female or feminine
fiesta *[fee-ess'-tah]* a celebration or party
hacienda *[ah-see-ehn'-dah]* ranch, country estate
huipil *[oo-ee-pihl']* traditional embroidered dress or blouse (plural: **huipiles**)
mescal *[mez'-cahl]* a strong alcoholic drink
morena *[moh-reh'-nah]* having brown skin and hair
tejocote *[teh-hoh-coh'-teh]* a type of hawthorn tree with yellow fruits
Virgen *[veer'-hehn]* a name for the Virgin Mary